The Old Man and the Cat

By

Anthony Holcroft

Illustrated by

Leah Palmer Preiss

PUFFIN BOOKS

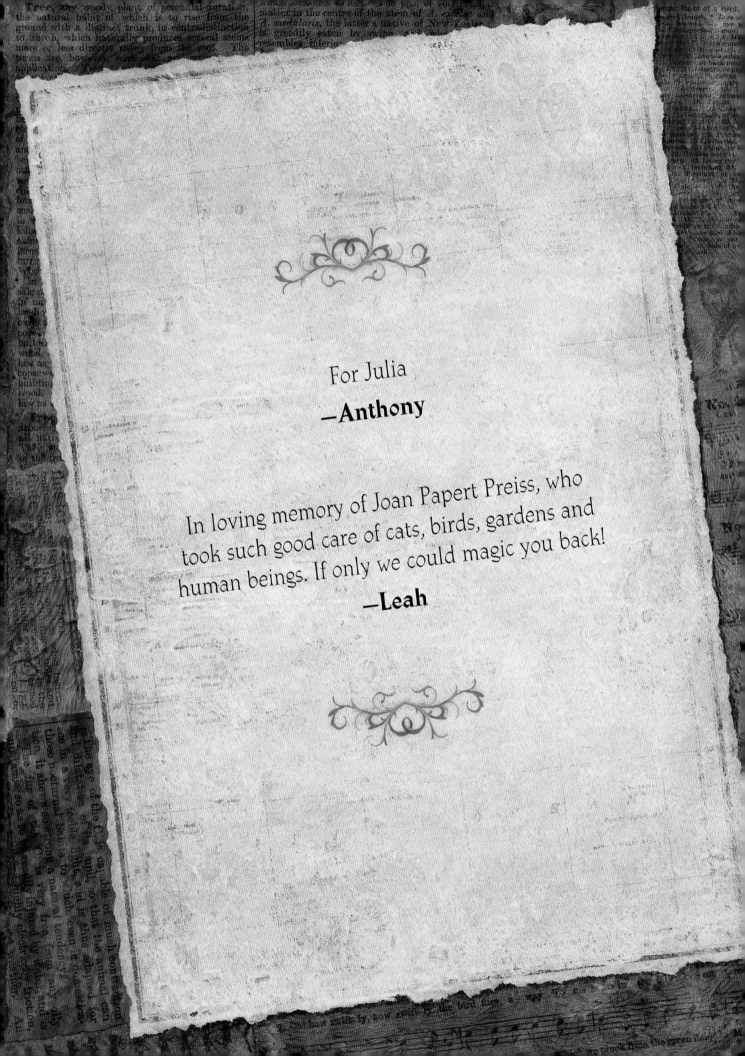

For Julia

—Anthony

In loving memory of Joan Papert Preiss, who took such good care of cats, birds, gardens and human beings. If only we could magic you back!

—Leah

nce, long ago, an old man lived alone on the edge of a forest. Near his house was a lake with an island, where many birds lived. Every morning and evening he walked along the shore and listened to their singing. *If only they would come and sit on my hands*, thought the old man, *then I could stroke them.* But the birds were timid and they never came near him.

On the shore of the island there grew a large leafy tree. In autumn bunches of berries hung like grapes from its branches. It was a favourite nesting place for the birds and sometimes the whole tree was black with them.

One night during a storm, the tree was struck down by lightning and the next day the old man found it washed up on his beach.

The wood was a warm honey-brown colour and very beautiful. It seemed a pity to use it for firewood. 'I will make something from it,' said the old man.

He began carving the wood with a knife.
At first he wasn't sure what to make, but
after a while he saw that the wood under
his knife was taking the shape of a flute.

When it was finished the flute glowed like a wand in the dusk. The old man put it to his lips and at once the flute seemed to play all on its own, as if someone else's fingers were touching it. The tune it played was slow and sad, and when the birds on the island heard it they flew to the old man in a big flock. They circled his head and perched on his arms and hands so that he was almost covered by a cloak of birds.

It grew dark, and the moon came up over the hill turning the lake into a silvery glass. And still the birds flew in shadowy circles around the old man's head. He put the flute down and the birds flew back to the island leaving him alone on the shore.

The old man was astonished and delighted by the magic flute he had made but he was also a little alarmed. *It is one thing to make a flute, he thought, but an enchanted one is another matter. Magic can get out of hand sometimes.*

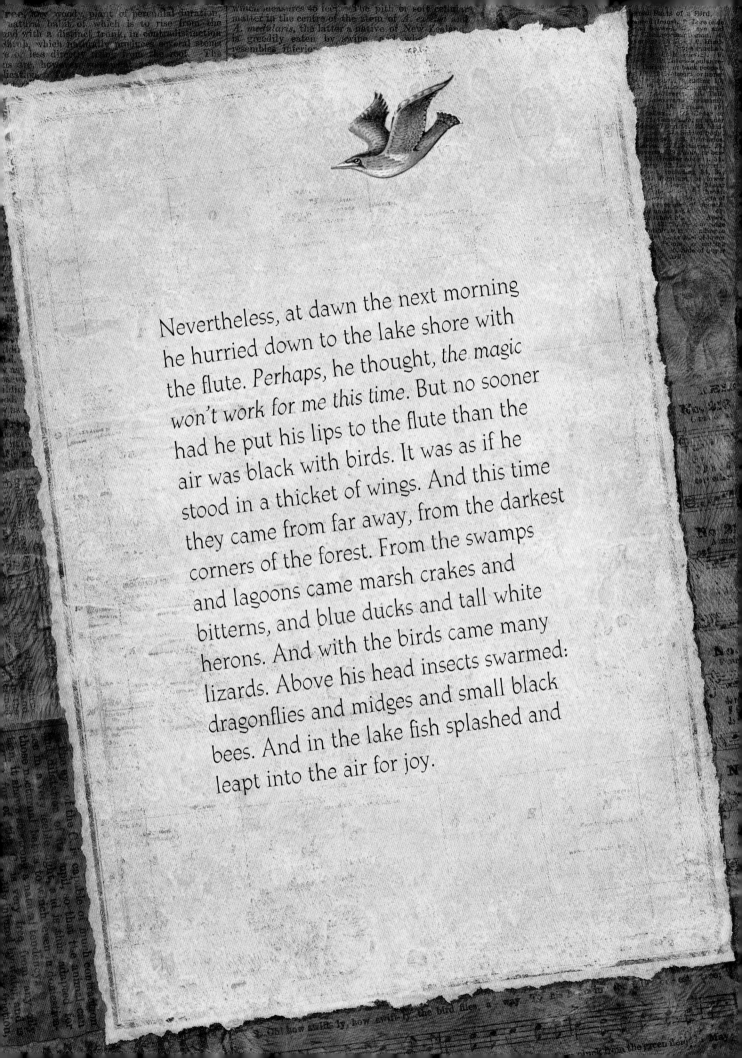

Nevertheless, at dawn the next morning he hurried down to the lake shore with the flute. *Perhaps, he thought, the magic won't work for me this time.* But no sooner had he put his lips to the flute than the air was black with birds. It was as if he stood in a thicket of wings. And this time they came from far away, from the darkest corners of the forest. From the swamps and lagoons came marsh crakes and bitterns, and blue ducks and tall white herons. And with the birds came many lizards. Above his head insects swarmed: dragonflies and midges and small black bees. And in the lake fish splashed and leapt into the air for joy.

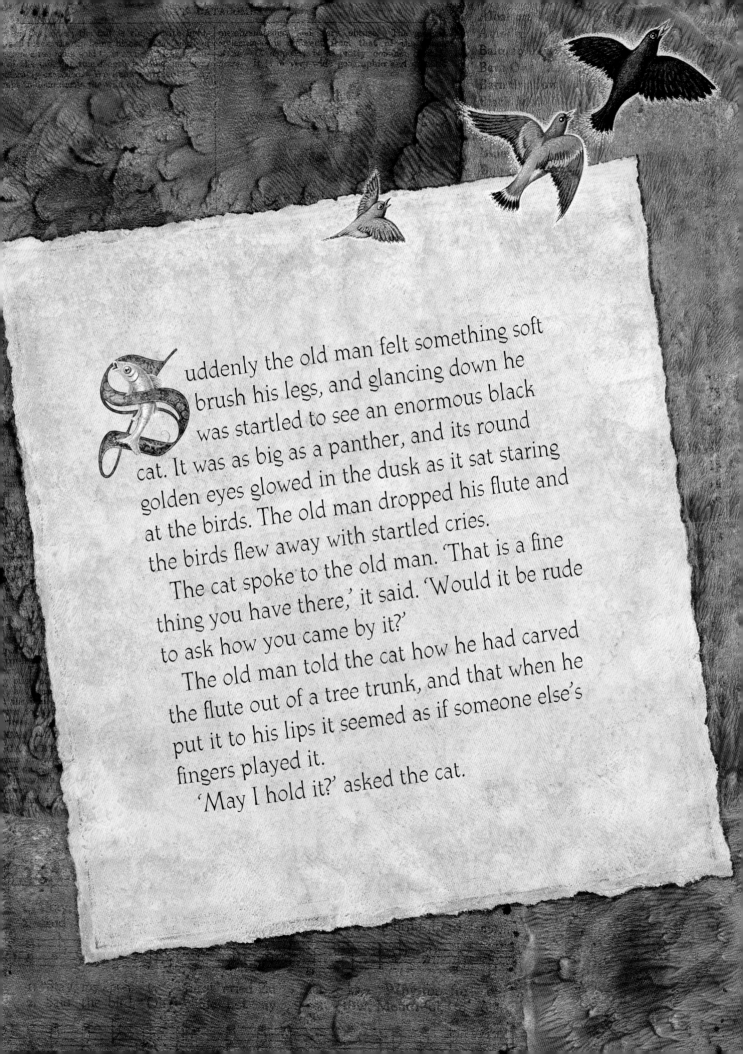

Suddenly the old man felt something soft brush his legs, and glancing down he was startled to see an enormous black cat. It was as big as a panther, and its round golden eyes glowed in the dusk as it sat staring at the birds. The old man dropped his flute and the birds flew away with startled cries.

The cat spoke to the old man. 'That is a fine thing you have there,' it said. 'Would it be rude to ask how you came by it?'

The old man told the cat how he had carved the flute out of a tree trunk, and that when he put it to his lips it seemed as if someone else's fingers played it.

'May I hold it?' asked the cat.

The old man hesitated for a moment. But then he thought, *no harm can come from letting him hold it.* So he gave the flute to the cat who at once put it to its lips and began to play. The forest creatures flocked to the cat just as they had to the old man, and all the time the cat sat quite still, staring at them with big golden eyes. At last the cat handed the flute back.

'Thank you, Old Man,' it said. 'Your flute sings very nicely.' And without another word it slipped away into the forest.

The old man walked back slowly to his house. He felt troubled. He did not like the way the black cat had stared at the birds with its greedy eyes, and the stealthy way in which it moved. Perhaps, even now, it was watching him from somewhere in the forest.

Before he went to sleep that night the old man put the flute beneath his pillow and for a long time lay with his fingers curled around it. When at last, just before dawn, he fell asleep, he saw the black cat in a dream, watching him from the top of a large leafy tree.

Suddenly the old man was wakened by a sound like a big wind. He stumbled outside to see a huge flock of birds disappearing like a storm cloud behind the hill.

Below him a grey mist hid the lake. Far away he heard a faint sound of a flute, like a bird crying. Then all was still. He ran back to his bed and flung aside the pillow. The flute was gone.

A year passed. The old man worked every day in his garden digging potatoes, gathering elderberries for wine and making blackberry jam. But now he did everything with a heavy heart. From dawn to dusk no birds sang. No lizards scuttled away from under the rocks and tussocks. No longer did the small grey moths sip honey at dusk from the bushes of golden cottonwood. The forest was silent and cold.

One evening, as the old man was walking wearily up the path to his house, he saw two golden eyes glowing at the edge of the forest. It was the black cat. It crawled towards him on its belly. Then slowly and painfully it got to its feet and crouched shivering in front of him. It had grown very thin. The fur hung in shreds from its ribs and its tail dragged along the ground. 'Old Man,' croaked the cat, 'I did an evil thing. I stole your flute while you were asleep and charmed away all the creatures of the forest.'

'Tell me what you did with them,' said the old man sternly.

The cat bowed its head. 'I put them in a big oven and cooked them. And afterwards there were no birds left anywhere in the forest. There were no lizards and no moths. There was nothing for me to eat. And so I starved until I had barely strength to crawl back to see you.'

'What do you want from me, Black Cat?' said the old man. 'I have nothing to give you.'

'I have come to ask you to forgive me,' said the cat. The old man looked at the cat and his anger turned to pity. 'Come with me,' he said.

He went into the house and put down on the floor a plate of bread soaked in milk. The cat swallowed the bread in one gulp. 'Thank you,' it whispered. 'Now go and look under your pillow, and you will find something there.'

The old man ran to his bed and threw
aside the pillow. There, glowing in the
darkness, lay his flute. 'Thank you!'
cried the old man. But the black cat had gone.
The old man hurried down to the lake to play
his flute. The sound echoed through the forest
and around the hills, but nothing stirred.

Not even a night beetle came buzzing through the warm still air.

'I will try one more time,' said the old man sadly. Once more he put the flute to his lips. At first he heard nothing. Then suddenly two small brown birds flew out of the forest and circled his head. The old man was delighted. *Perhaps more will come,* he thought.

And indeed, the next morning several birds came to the call of his flute, and with them came a handful of moths and a pair of slim green lizards. At last, after a week, there were enough birds to waken the old man in the morning with their singing. And for the first time in a year there were bees in his flowers and wasps in his ripe fruit. The old man was overjoyed.

Yet one thing still clouded his happiness. Suppose one day the flute should once again be stolen from him — what a terrible thing that would be. *The forest has its family back again,* he thought. *It is very nice to have an enchanted flute. But magic can be dangerous.*

He made a big fire of brushwood on the beach, and when it was red-hot, he threw the flute into the middle of it and watched until it had burned to ashes.

Without the flute the birds no longer flew around the old man's head. And no longer did the lizards dart over his feet or the moths flutter in the palm of his hand. But the birds still woke him every morning with their singing and the lizards still scuttled underneath the stones, and in the evening the moths fluttered from flower to flower.

And it pleased the old man to know that they were there.

PUFFIN BOOKS
Published by the Penguin Group
Penguin Group (NZ), 67 Apollo Drive, Rosedale,
Auckland 0632, New Zealand (a division of Pearson New Zealand Ltd)
Penguin Group (USA) Inc., 375 Hudson Street,
New York, New York 10014, USA
Penguin Group (Canada), 90 Eglinton Avenue East, Suite 700, Toronto,
Ontario, M4P 2Y3, Canada (a division of Pearson Penguin Canada Inc.)
Penguin Books Ltd, 80 Strand, London, WC2R 0RL, England
Penguin Ireland, 25 St Stephen's Green,
Dublin 2, Ireland (a division of Penguin Books Ltd)
Penguin Group (Australia), 250 Camberwell Road, Camberwell,
Victoria 3124, Australia (a division of Pearson Australia Group Pty Ltd)
Penguin Books India Pvt Ltd, 11, Community Centre,
Panchsheel Park, New Delhi – 110 017, India
Penguin Books (South Africa) (Pty) Ltd, Block D, Rosebank Office Park,
181 Jan Smuts Avenue, Parktown North, Gauteng 2193, South Africa

Penguin Books Ltd, Registered Offices: 80 Strand, London, WC2R 0RL, England

The Old Man and the Cat first published by Whitcoulls Publishers, 1984
This edition published by Puffin Books, 2012
1 3 5 7 9 10 8 6 4 2

Text copyright © Anthony Holcroft, 1984
Illustrations copyright © Leah Palmer Preiss, 2012

The right of Anthony Holcroft and Leah Palmer Preiss to be
identified as the author and illustrator of this work in terms of
section 96 of the Copyright Act 1994 is hereby asserted.
All rights reserved

Designed and typeset by Mark Glover
Prepress by Image Centre Ltd
Printed in China through Bookbuilders, Hong Kong

All rights reserved. Without limiting the rights under copyright reserved
above, no part of this publication may be reproduced, stored in or
introduced into a retrieval system, or transmitted, in any form or by any
means (electronic, mechanical, photocopying, recording or otherwise),
without the prior written permission of both the copyright owner and
the above publisher of this book.

ISBN 978-0-143-50464-1

A catalogue record for this book is available
from the National Library of New Zealand.

www.penguin.co.nz